Additional Dragonblade Books by Author Mary Lancaster

One Night in Blackhaven Series
The Captain's Old Love (Book 1)
The Earl's Promised Bride (Book 2)
The Soldier's Impossible Love (Book 3)
The Gambler's Last Chance (Book 4)
The Poet's Stern Critic (Book 5)
The Rake's Mistake (Book 6)

The Duel Series
Entangled (Book 1)
Captured (Book 2)
Deserted (Book 3)
Beloved (Book 4)
Haunted (Novella)

Last Flame of Alba Series
Rebellion's Fire (Book 1)
A Constant Blaze (Book 2)
Burning Embers (Book 3)

Gentlemen of Pleasure Series
The Devil and the Viscount (Book 1)
Temptation and the Artist (Book 2)
Sin and the Soldier (Book 3)
Debauchery and the Earl (Book 4)
Blue Skies (Novella)

Pleasure Garden Series
Unmasking the Hero (Book 1)

Unmasking Deception (Book 2)
Unmasking Sin (Book 3)
Unmasking the Duke (Book 4)
Unmasking the Thief (Book 5)

Crime & Passion Series
Mysterious Lover (Book 1)
Letters to a Lover (Book 2)
Dangerous Lover (Book 3)
Lost Lover (Book 4)
Merry Lover (Novella)
Ghostly Lover (Novella)

The Husband Dilemma Series
How to Fool a Duke (Book 1)

Season of Scandal Series
Pursued by the Rake (Book 1)
Abandoned to the Prodigal (Book 2)
Married to the Rogue (Book 3)
Unmasked by her Lover (Book 4)
Her Star from the East (Novella)

Imperial Season Series
Vienna Waltz (Book 1)
Vienna Woods (Book 2)
Vienna Dawn (Book 3)

Blackhaven Brides Series
The Wicked Baron (Book 1)
The Wicked Lady (Book 2)
The Wicked Rebel (Book 3)
The Wicked Husband (Book 4)
The Wicked Marquis (Book 5)
The Wicked Governess (Book 6)
The Wicked Spy (Book 7)

The Wicked Gypsy (Book 8)
The Wicked Wife (Book 9)
Wicked Christmas (Book 10)
The Wicked Waif (Book 11)
The Wicked Heir (Book 12)
The Wicked Captain (Book 13)
The Wicked Sister (Book 14)

Unmarriageable Series
The Deserted Heart (Book 1)
The Sinister Heart (Book 2)
The Vulgar Heart (Book 3)
The Broken Heart (Book 4)
The Weary Heart (Book 5)
The Secret Heart (Book 6)
Christmas Heart (Novella)

The Lyon's Den Series
Fed to the Lyon

De Wolfe Pack: The Series
The Wicked Wolfe
Vienna Wolfe

Also from Mary Lancaster
Madeleine (Novella)
The Others of Ochil (Novella)

Chapter One

George's hired chaise lost a wheel some three miles from the next posting inn. Since the sky was already beginning to darken with both storm clouds and dusk, he chose not to shelter in the wrecked carriage, but to take his bag and walk on to the inn, from where he would send help back to the postilions and the horses.

Tired as he was, George enjoyed the walk. Since deciding to come home from his travels, he seemed to have spent far too much of his time cooped up in carriages, and his body appreciated the opportunity to stretch. However, he doubted he would appreciate the soaking once the storm clouds broke, so he strode on at a cracking pace.

Even so, he could hear thunder rumbling away in the distance, and the rain came on before he could have been more than halfway there.

The posting inn was on the edge of a village. It was not hard to find in the dark, since the racket of voices, music, and laughter penetrated the battering of the rain on his hat, and even the louder rumbles of thunder.

The inn was so packed that at first no one noticed his quiet entrance. The taproom seemed to have overflowed into the coffee room. A fiddler was scraping away in one corner. A few young women were screaming with laughter from the laps of young gentlemen. A cockfight appeared to be taking place in the middle of the room, surrounded by raucous gentlemen yelling encouragement to the birds and waving money around. In fact, for such a large crowd, it seemed to have a disproportionate number of gentlemen to more ordinary country folk and travelers of other classes.

George did not care for crowds, particularly of the unexpected and disorganized variety. The flying feathers and blood made him feel sick. He had to hold on to his purpose quite hard to force himself to stay. He took off his hat, gripping it far too hard. The sea of noise was overwhelming enough to drown him.

From the depths of the heaving masses, a harassed-looking man in an apron, a feather clinging to his hair, squeezed through to him.

"Evening, sir. Can I help you?"

"My post-chaise lost a wheel three miles back on the Dover Road. The postillions need help to get the horses and the vehicle to the inn. I require a room for the night and dinner."

If anything, the innkeeper looked even more harassed. "I'll send a couple of ostlers to do what they can. Your postillions can bed down in the stables with the grooms. But as for a private bedchamber, sir, I couldn't do it if my life depended on it." He flapped one hand around the chaos. "There's a prizefight in the neighborhood tomorrow, and it's brought all the quality down from London and God knows where else. To say nothing of the hordes of lesser men. I like business as much as the next innkeeper, but this is ridiculous! My wife will be after blood—*more* blood, and probably mine!—when she finds they're holding cockfights in here..."

It was a long time since anything had panicked George, but he could feel it rising up from his toes now.

"When will they go to bed?"

"Half of them ain't got beds," the innkeeper said. "They'll have to sleep here, which I admit I wouldn't care for myself."

"Neither would I," George said, desperation clamoring. "Can you offer me nothing else? Discomfort I will live with, but it has to be private."

"I got nothing like that, sir. Even my own servants are bunking in together, and my whole family's in one room. I can ask if anyone will give up their chamber for a gentleman, but I tell you now, I wouldn't hold my breath." Perhaps he read the panic in George's face, for he turned hastily to the nearest table. "Here, anyone like to give this poor, soaked gentleman their bed and sleep down here?"

"Not me, I'm going home to my Jenny," rumbled a countryman.

A traveler of indeterminate rank shook his head furiously. "Sorry, friend, not for the king himself! I was here first, and here I stay."

"Perhaps there is another hostelry in the area?" George said, trying to think through the noise.

"Not round here, no," the innkeeper said. "And to be honest, I doubt anyone in the village will open their doors to a stranger. But you're welcome to kip down here for nothing—dinner and breakfast half price."

"I'd rather sleep outside in the rain." It was truth, if vaguely insulting to the innkeeper, so George hoped he hadn't said it aloud.

"Oh, I don't know," the countryman said with a grin George didn't quite like. "There's Hazel House. Loads of space up there. I'm sure the widow'd be happy to look after a gentleman."

"Ain't no call for that, Jack," the innkeeper scolded, though George had no idea why.

"What?" Jack demanded innocently.

George didn't care. "A lodging house? Where do I find it?"

"Straight through the village and take the right fork," Jack said helpfully. A man on his other side grinned and nudged him. George saw it but was too upset to analyze the meaning.

"Good half-hour's walk or more, though," the innkeeper warned, glaring at Jack and his friend. "You'll get soaked in this weather. If the lightning doesn't get you. And she'll likely not let you stay, anyway."

But George, eager to be away from the inn, was already making for the door, calling over his shoulder, "You won't forget to send someone to help with the post-chaise and horses?"

"No, it's in hand, sir, but..."

George waited for no more. He almost crashed through the inn's front door in his haste to leave. For an instant, the pleasure of having the barrier of stone and wood between him and the noise and the sea of raucous strangers was intense. Rain pattered on his head. He put his hat back on, and water ran off the brim and down the back of his neck. He shivered and set off through the village.

The thunder rumbled closer. The rain was about to get heavier.

※

THUNDER CRASHED JUST as Francesca parted the curtains to let Mark see out the window. The boy jumped with excitement and climbed on to the window seat to peer into the darkness.

"I can't see anything!" he said, disappointed, while the thunderclap rumbled away into silence. "Just rain on the glass."

"In a few moments, you'll probably see some lightning in the sky, like a flash, and then you have to count until the thunder sounds to tell how far away the storm is." Francesca tried to keep her voice calm, since she didn't want to communicate her own foolish fear of thunderstorms to her son. What she really wanted to do was hide them both under a thick blanket and stick her fingers in her ears.

But she forced herself to sit on the window seat while Mark stood beside her, avidly waiting. It wasn't long. Lightning flashed, sudden and ominous, illuminating the figure of a man near the window.

Francesca gasped and leapt up, whisking Mark off the seat.

"Did you see the man?" he asked, wriggling excitedly. "Was it Papa?"

The clatter of thunder prevented her having to answer. *Of course it was not Papa. Papa has been dead for more than two years, half of your life.* She never wanted him to forget his father, but nor did she want him to imagine him in every shadow or stranger lurking in the garden...

Why was a stranger in the garden in the midst of a storm? On foot, shoulders hunched against the battering rain, moving quickly and purposefully...

The thunder quietened again into a much closer, insistent knocking.

Her breath caught. Mark realized it at the same time.

"Someone's at the door!" He broke free of her, rushing across the room. "It *is* Papa!"

"Marco, it isn't." The words stuck in her throat as she started after him.

Lightning flashed again, followed by an almost immediate bang of thunder that made her jump almost out of her skin. By the time she could move, Mark was out of the room. She hurried after him into the hall, snatching up the nearest candlestick on her way.

At once, a blast of cold air hit her, along with the too-loud pelting of the rain on the ground outside. The candles flickered crazily.

In front of Mark's tiny figure, the front door stood open and the dark, threatening figure of a man stepped into the house. He slammed the door behind him.

Francesca flew forward to grasp Mark by the shoulder. Just touching him felt like a massive relief, but she still had the stranger to deal with. He turned, dripping, to face her. She raised the candle higher to glare at him.

He *was* a stranger, too tall, too masculine, and far too much in her house. He stood still, a large, wet bag and beaver hat grasped in one hand, gazing from Mark to her. Rain streamed off the capes of his greatcoat like a small waterfall. In the candlelight, the hair at his temples glinted silver. His face was unreadable but did not appear immediately threatening.

"You're not Papa," Mark said.

"No, I'm not anyone's papa," the man agreed. His voice was a little hoarse, perhaps from the weather, or from surprise, and yet gave an impression of vagueness. But his eyes, lifting to Francesca's once more, were remarkably clear and direct.

"You have no business here," Francesca said icily. Where the devil was Martin? Not that he would strike fear into anyone's heart.

"No. Forgive me," the stranger said. At least he sounded like a gentleman. "The boy let me in, and I'm afraid I was so wet I didn't wait for further invitation."

Words stuck in her throat. Should she betray vulnerability by saying, *My son and I are alone, apart from two ancient servants, so you have to go?* Or simply, rudely, command him to leave?

One should not send a dog out in such weather. And the stranger was already soaked to the skin.

"You cannot stay here," she said, more annoyed with the situation than with him.

Besides, even as she said the words, she realized how powerless she was to enforce them. He was bigger, stronger, and all of her haughtiness could not compensate for the fact that behind her stood only a doddery elderly couple. And even they must be asleep.

An expression of resignation crossed the man's face. He inclined his head, picked up his sodden bag from the floor where he had dropped it, and turned to the front door, reaching for the latch. Water spilled off his hair, down his neck, over his gloves. He was shivering with cold.

"He *could* be Papa," Mark said doubtfully.

He could not, of course, and he wasn't. But Percival had been a traveler in his time, too, caught in many a storm. And this man clearly was about to go as she bade him.

"Wait," she said, before she could think, let alone talk herself out of it. "Why did you come *here?*"

"They said in the village you might have room. The inn is packed to the gunnels, and I could not face spending the night in the coffee room with hordes of strange drunks."

She swallowed, keeping her gaze on his face and hoping she wasn't about to make the worst mistake of her life. "Mark, go and fetch Martin. He won't have heard the door for the noise of the thunder."

Mark grinned and ran off. He was too starved of company not to welcome a stranger. There was guilt in that, but mostly she was concerned with the traveler.

She glanced at his sodden bag. At least it appeared to be made of leather. "Have you dry clothes in there?"

"I hope so."

"If they are damp, Martin will bring you something of my husband's. He will show you to a room to change, and then you had better come to the drawing room. There is at least a fire there. Martin will show you the way," she added, to make sure he understood he would not be left alone to wander the house.

"Thank you." He slid his hand off the latch with unmistakable relief.

"Give me your hat and your coat," she commanded.

Obediently, he peeled them off, but hung them on the empty hooks on the coat stand instead.

Mark bounced back through the baize door with Martin wheezing behind him. They had come so quickly that she knew Martin must already have been halfway up the stairs when Mark found him.

"Martin, be so good as to show this gentleman to the spare room. Lend him anything of Mr. Hazel's that he might need. Then bring him to the drawing room."

"Yes, ma'am," Martin replied, scowling at her, though whether because of the effort required or her admission of a strange man to the house, she could not tell.

The stranger meekly followed the old man upstairs, carrying his own bag. Thunder rumbled into the distance.

Francesca took the dripping beaver hat from its hook and passed it to Mark before lifting the overcoat, heavy with moisture. "We'll take these to the kitchen to dry," she said, and Mark happily followed her back down again.

There, she asked Ada to make tea while she hung the overcoat close to the kitchen stove. Hastily, she made a few sandwiches under Ada Martin's glower and carried the tray up to the drawing room herself.

She was only just in time. She heard Martin's slow tread on the stairs, and then a murmur of voices before quick, sure footsteps across the hall floor. A knock sounded on the drawing room door.

"Come in!" Mark called cheerfully.

The stranger entered with a somehow endearing lack of certainty. Too much arrogance, or even self-confidence, would have appalled her just then and probably sent her from the room, dragging Mark in her wake. But despite the man's gentlemanly posture and clearly excellent clothing, his expression was apologetic and wary.

In fact, it came to her that he was anxious.

"Forgive me. I was mistaken," he said.

His hasty speech calmed her further. "Sit down and tell me how, over tea. Take the chair nearest the fire—you must be chilled to the bone. Do you like your tea with cream and sugar?"

"Just sugar, thank you." He took the cup from her with a nod that was almost a bow and took himself off to the opposite chair. Mark gazed at him with an interest that did not appear to disconcert him—at least not any further.

The stranger said, "I thought from the way the men spoke at the inn that this was some kind of rooming house. It is clearly no such thing. I can only beg your pardon for disturbing you. Is it improper for me to stay here?"

Francesca sighed. "I think you were misled rather than mistaken, sir."

His eyebrows flew up. "Deliberately? Why?"

"I am foreign. I have no husband to protect me, and they choose to think the worst. I believe you were not meant to believe me the landlady of a rooming house, but rather a merry widow who welcomes the company of single gentlemen."

The stranger blushed, which enchanted her.

"I am glad the possibility did not cross your mind," she said frankly. "Or I really would throw you out in the storm."

"Perhaps you should anyway. It is already lessening, and if you are alone here apart from servants…"

Mark laughed. "Don't be silly. She has me!"

"That must be a great comfort to her," the stranger said gravely.

"What's your name?" Mark asked him. "I'm Mark, though Mama calls me Marco sometimes."

"George." The stranger set his cup and saucer on the table beside him and delved into his pocket. Holding a visiting card between his fingers, he leaned over to offer it to Francesca. "I meant to give you this when I came in."

Sir Arthur Astley, she read. *Denholm Hall, St. Bride's, Lincolnshire.*

Slowly, she lifted her gaze from the card to his face. "You just told my son your name is George."

"George is my middle name. My friends use it. But I am officially Sir Arthur."

This time it was she who blushed, at being over suspicious. "Francesca Hazel," she murmured, and inhaled too quickly as a clap of thunder sounded closer once more. At least she did not jump or spill her tea. Sir Arthur's brows twitched as though he had noticed her reaction, but he said nothing.

"My papa is Percival Hazel," Mark informed him proudly. "He was a great violinist and composer, but he died."

"I'm very sorry," Sir Arthur said sincerely, although in truth, Mark hadn't sounded remotely sad. He didn't, as a rule. "I have heard of him, of course."

"Perhaps you heard him play?" Francesca said.

"Sadly not." He seemed to feel something more was called for, because he added, "I have been away a good deal."

"Abroad?" Francesca asked, hoping he had been to Italy.

"Some of the time."

"Of course it was difficult for him to play in Europe during the war, but with the peace of 1814, he played in Paris and Vienna, and all over Italy. But he felt obliged to take us home when Bonaparte escaped."

"I did not go abroad until 1815," Sir Arthur said. "Just before Waterloo."

Curious timing. She did not say so aloud.

"I am returning home from Africa," he offered.

Her eyes widened. "What took you there?"

"Curiosity. I went to Egypt, originally, to see the tombs. I would have stayed longer, but I have responsibilities at home."

"Of course. Have a sandwich. Tell me about Egypt."

He began a little hesitantly, as if unsure what, if anything, she actually wanted to hear, but after she asked a couple of questions, and Mark expressed amazement, his natural enthusiasm seemed to carry him away. He spoke well, with considerable knowledge, a deep understanding, and occasional subtle humor that she almost missed. She found herself transported under the burning sun, among people of wildly different customs and beliefs, swept back into a past that was both fascinating and frightening.

Because she was so spellbound, it was some time before she noticed that Mark had apparently lost interest. He had wandered off to the sofa nearer the window and was sitting smiling, as though at something or someone she could not see.

Her stomach gave one of its uneasy twinges.

Mark laughed. "No, I like him. He's funny."

Sir Arthur stopped talking and glanced at Marco, then back to

Francesca, who smiled faintly.

"He's playing," she said, hoping it was true.

Mark slid off the sofa and ran up to Sir Arthur. Taking him by the hand, he tugged. "Come and meet my papa!"

Chapter Two

GEORGE HAD JUST got comfortable. Warm and dry, in quiet, pleasant surroundings, with warm tea and food in his belly and the company of a gentle, beautiful young woman. She seemed so interested in his stories that he had almost forgotten they were strangers. He liked to make her smile, to watch the array of expressions cross her face and know she understood. He liked her voice too, low and musical and intriguingly accented.

And then the boy seized his hand. "Come and meet my papa!"

George kept his gaze on the boy, holding on to her words, *He's playing*, that he did not quite believe. They had all said "Papa" was dead. The men at the inn who had called her a widow, Mark, Mrs. Hazel herself. Was he being fooled in some way again?

It did not happen often, and he had taught himself to recognize the flim-flam men and women, the liars and the cheats. There weren't many of them, and he had felt no such alarm bells with her.

The boy was smiling, but his eyes were serious. He really wanted George to meet someone. Without looking at Mrs. Hazel, he rose and let Mark lead him to the sofa.

"This is my papa," the boy said proudly. "Papa, this is George, who was caught in the storm. We're letting him stay because he is kind."

George looked where the boy was looking—at the back of the sofa—and felt a little frisson of memory, one deeply buried in his own childhood. Showing a very different adult someone no one else in the room could see. And just for a moment, he imagined he *did* see a man sitting on the sofa—a misty, insubstantial figure with wild, merry eyes and a sensitive mouth. He shivered, and the illusion vanished.

Mark laughed. "Papa says you had better be, but he is only joking. I can tell he likes you."

"Enough, Marco," his mother interrupted, as though she were trying not to speak too sharply. "It is past time for bed, and the storm is quieter. Say goodnight to Sir George."

For some reason, the name surprised him. People either called him Sir Arthur, or just George, depending on when and how they knew him. He wasn't quite sure why he had told the boy he was called George, except that there was an honesty in such young children, and George was more closely related to who he was. Sir Arthur was who he had become, the miracle that enabled him to travel where he willed, meet interesting people, learn from more than just books, make decisions. But at heart, he was still George.

"Good night, Sir George!" Mark said enthusiastically.

George smiled. "I feel I should be slaying dragons when you call me that. Good night."

"Can I help slay the dragons?" Mark asked over his shoulder as his mother led him from the room.

"Of course. You shall be my apprentice."

Mark grinned at him, in clear expectation of an exciting new game. But it was Francesca's smile that stunned him. Part amused, part grateful, it softened her watchful, anxious eyes and made them sparkle. Her whole being lit up with a beauty that deprived him of breath.

Fortunately, she turned away from him, so she couldn't have begun to suspect the effect of her mere smile upon him.

Mere? There was nothing mere about it.

George liked to look at beauty. Beautiful women were no exception, but they did not usually tongue-tie him. Some of his closest friends were beautiful women—Lady Hera, for example, his first true friend who had shown him the way to freedom and truth.

But this girl, this mother, was nothing like Hera. Nor any of the women who had moved him since. She was a widow, the wife of a great musician, yet someone the villagers had felt free to play unkind tricks on. He should not be here, threatening her already precarious reputation, and yet the many layers and facets of her character fascinated him.

Of course, he was given to obsessions. Once he had solved the puzzle or revealed everything to his own satisfaction, he was usually prepared to move on to the next. For this woman's safety, he should move on *now*.

He was pacing between the shuttered window and a large, beautiful pianoforte that he had barely noticed before. He used it now as a quite deliberate distraction, running his hand over the smooth, polished curves, depressing the occasional key to appreciate the tone and timbre of a single note, perfectly in tune.

"Do you play, Sir Arthur?"

Her voice from the doorway took him by surprise. He realized he was sorry not to be Sir George to her still.

"No." He straightened. "I never learned. The pianoforte was always in the drawing room. But I like to listen."

She looked slightly confused by that but did not ask anything, for which he was grateful. He did not want to say to her, *I was an odd child who embarrassed my parents in front of guests, so they kept me hidden, pretending I was ill and then dead.* "Do you play?" he asked hastily.

"Sometimes." Another flash of lightning penetrated the room, and her breath caught. Her shoulders tensed as she waited for the crash of thunder. "I used to be quite good."

"Used to be?" He frowned. The rumble of thunder was quite distant, and she relaxed visibly.

"Yes. I used to play all the time. Now, I need to be in a certain mood. One has to practice constantly to keep the skill honed."

Something slotted into place in his mind. "You were a player, like your husband."

She tilted her head with a hint of defiance, daring him to criticize. "It was how I met him. We performed at the same theatre in Naples, and then played together many times."

"But his death changed everything for you," he guessed.

"Of course. But playing was already difficult by then."

"Why?" he asked.

Her body jerked, very slightly, as though she would turn away from him, and he knew he had been too blunt. But before he could apologize, she said in a rush, "War. Guns and panic that cleared the concert hall. Soldiers on the rampage, shooting everywhere. Now I need peace in order to play." She stared at him, clearly appalled by her own words. "I'm sorry. I didn't mean to say that, and you didn't wish to hear it. Your honesty is catching."

She snatched her hand off the piano, as though afraid it would shake, and from impulse he caught it, holding it lightly but firmly, wishing only to comfort, because he too had been lonely and frightened in his life. Her fingers were soft and slender. They jumped in his, and then, before he could release her and apologize, they gripped his hand hard while thunder rumbled off into the distance.

"I have met soldiers who can longer bear the sound of guns," he said. "Or thunder. What happened to you?"

"Nothing. I hid beneath a harpsicord in a store cupboard until they were gone. Percival found me there. But I never forgot the fear, or the grief, because I thought I would never see him again. And now I never will."

"Does Mark see him? Or is he really just playing?"

Her eyes widened. She seemed to have forgotten her hand resting in his. Her mouth, curiously vulnerable, opened to speak and then closed again.

Slowly, she drew her hand free. "He imagines he does. As though wishing would make it true." She moved toward the sofa and sat down, almost exactly where Mark had been staring.

"Can he still remember what he looks like?" George asked.

"He seems to. He knew you were not Percival as soon as he saw you clearly, but he hopes. He is lonely."

He was not, George thought sadly, the only one. "Because the villagers are cruel?"

She nodded once.

"What is their problem with you? Just because you are *different* to them?"

"That and…the vicar's wife cut me when she realized I had played in public for money. *On the stage like a common actress,* I believe were her precise words." She shrugged. "Often, the ordinary people take their cues from those they imagine are their betters. While Percival was alive, it was not so bad, but after his death, their hostility grew more open. Now I hear words like *foreign whore* spoken quite openly when I walk into the village. For myself, I don't really care, but what if Mark hears and understands?"

George was appalled. "Intolerable!" He threw himself down on the sofa beside her. "Who is the magistrate?"

"I will not involve the law and allow such accusations to be official."

He closed his mouth, swallowing down his objections. He saw her dilemma, whatever the injustice. "So what *will* you do?"

"Pretend I do not hear or care. Show that they will never frighten me."

He met her gaze. "Do they?"

"Not when I do not care. I do not want to care."

"Not to care is not to be alive."

A frown flickered across her face and vanished, but he thought he had irritated her. "What or who do you care about, Sir Arthur, called

George?"

He could not help smiling. "Many things now—many people that I once did not even know about."

She studied him until his eyes slid away. He liked her too much already to be comfortable with her displeasure.

But she did not sound displeased, just curious. "You are a little unworldly, are you not?"

"Yes," he admitted. "I am only just discovering it. In reality, I mean. I feel like a very well-educated child."

"Why? What is your story, Sir George? What dragons have you slain?"

"Internal ones, largely."

"You don't want to tell me," she said shrewdly. "Even though I have told you my secrets."

"Not all of them. But you are right. I am wary of contempt."

She looked gratifyingly startled. "Do you deserve it?"

"My friends would say not." From the corner of his eye, some movement distracted him, but when he glanced around, there was nothing there but the flickering candles. He felt again the shiver of memory, of an old, long-buried sensitivity.

"Someone walked over your grave," she observed. "A peculiar English saying."

"It is," he agreed, and began a humorous debate on the derivation of the phrase. It made her laugh, as he intended, and for a little they happily compared English, Latin, and modern Italian oddities.

Inevitably, the conversation broadened and led down unexpected paths that were both intriguing and fun. Until he realized there had been no thunder for an hour and the rain had receded. He rose with strange reluctance and bowed.

"Once again, my thanks for your kindness and for your company this evening. I will bid you goodnight."

"Goodnight," she responded, standing with him. "But if there was any kindness on my part, I believe you have repaid it."

"I wish I could." He wanted to take her hand and kiss it, but in the circumstances, it would have been highly inappropriate. Even less appropriate than imposing on her hospitality unchaperoned.

Since there was nothing else to do, he walked away and crossed the hall to the stairs, where he lit one of the small candles and found his way back to the bedchamber in which he had changed.

A fire had been lit there, taking the chill off the wet autumn evening, an additional thoughtfulness he had not expected from the ancient manservant. Wondering about her life here, about her son and her talented late husband, he prepared for bed.

Only as he was about to blow out the final candle and lay his head on the pillow did he become aware of the tension within the room.

George was sensitive to what he thought of as "atmosphere," stemming from his childhood, when he had so often failed to understand people or the expressions behind their words. Instead, he had relied on undercurrents that he could not name, until he had found his way back to the safety of his own comfortable space.

Only much later had he come to understand that the safety lay not in the physical room but in himself. Curiosity had outweighed fear and false duty, enabling him to consider many more thoughts and actions and begin to live as he always should have. However, some atmospheres were still best avoided—like the raucous inn—because they jangled his nerves in acute discomfort.

There was no noise in the bedchamber except his own breathing, the rustling of the bedclothes, the occasional gentle movement of the glowing coal in the guarded fireplace. And yet there was hostility here. Like his father's when he was disappointed. Like Nurse when she could not get her gin, or his brother Hugh when the numbers did not go as he wanted them to. And yet there was no one but George in the room.

So who was angry with him?

His skin prickled. Was someone else in the room? One of the two servants? Mark?

No. No one had come in—the door creaked, and he would have heard. He was alone.

But he did sense *something*: a presence, an emotion, perhaps? Strong emotion.

A breeze blew over his skin, raising the hair on his arms and his head. He almost leapt out of bed, except that he could see from the glow of the coal there was no one else in the room.

Old houses were drafty.

He closed his eyes and tried to relax. He could hear music. A violin, playing something wild yet elegant. Vivaldi? He smiled because it must have been Francesca, even though her favored instrument was not the violin but the pianoforte.

His eyes flew open. Francesca had gone to her own chamber. He had heard her footsteps on the stairs and the passage, the closing of her bedroom door. The music was not loud, but it did not come from the room below, *or* from a room along the passage. It sounded too close, too intimate, in this very room…

Or perhaps just in his head. Was he as mad as his father had claimed?

The music was beautiful, the playing exquisite, and yet it came with some kind of threat. Anger. A warning. He stared toward the glow in the fireplace.

"Percival," he murmured.

The fire flared into a single flame that quickly died. And just for an instant, a man's figure seemed to form in the darkness, wispy and insubstantial.

"I won't hurt her," George said. "I won't hurt either of them."

Abruptly, the atmosphere eased, and the imagined figure vanished as though it had never been—which it probably hadn't. George was alone in a warm, comfortable room. Even the wind no longer howled outside, and the rain was gentle, intermittent against the window-panes.

He felt foolish, talking to an imaginary ghost. And yet in some ways it made sense that something of Percival lingered in this house, watching over his wife and child. It was as if Percival had identified himself to George with the music—however that was even possible—and made his warning plain. If George had intended any action against anyone in the house, he would undoubtedly have dropped it.

As it was, he felt a touch of guilt, because his attraction to Francesca was strong, and shame, because he was in danger of believing in the impossible.

Chapter Three

Francesca lay awake for some time, thinking about her strangely appealing guest.

She liked his serious expression and his sudden, sweet smile. She liked his instinctive kindness and the way he focused on what she—or Mark—said. She liked that he never imposed.

And, if she was strictly honest, she liked the way he looked, with his bronzed skin and his distinguished, handsome features. From the slight graying of the hair at his temples, she guessed he was around forty years old, a little older than her, pleasingly mature and yet with an air of almost childlike innocence.

The admiration she read in his eyes had surprised her but not frightened her. And he had taken no liberties apart from holding her hand once, and that had been comfort, not attempted seduction. He seemed very open and blunt, and yet mysterious too. She knew he was hiding something about his past.

Well, everyone was entitled to privacy. She had not needed to tell him about her fear of thunder and its association with the theatre attack... She had never told anyone before. She and Percival had rarely even discussed it because it came so close to separating them forever. Percival expressed himself through music, and he had cared deeply. But he had been too selfish to be very observant.

George had *noticed* her fear, and he had seemed to admire rather than judge, understand rather than pretend. And curiously, it helped. Had he stayed talking to her merely to distract her, out of kindness?

She liked kindness. But for the first time since Percival's death, she wanted to be *liked*. To be admired as a man admired a woman. She wanted George to desire her as, God help her, she desired him. Which was highly dangerous in the circumstances.

But she had been a widow for two years, and she could not help the stirrings of her body or her odd tug of attraction to the intriguing stranger. She savored the feeling, reveling in the secret heat spreading through her body, imagining his kiss, the touch of his hands…the intimate, deliciously physical loving she had known only with Percival.

George would be a different kind of lover, gentler, sweeter, with all the understanding and self-control of maturity. He would seek her pleasure always… Her body began to throb, making her shift restlessly, tangling her limbs in the sheets.

How wonderful would it be to seduce him from that self-discipline, just occasionally?

She gasped at the sudden ferocity of need—and Mark's laughter rang out, instantly dousing the foolish fantasy. She leapt out of bed and felt her way to the connecting door to Mark's room. A night light was always left there, burning very low. In its faint glow, Mark was sitting up against the pillows, grinning at something at the foot of his bed. He laughed again, turning his happy gaze toward Francesca.

"Look, Papa! Mama is here and can answer for herself."

Pain twisted through her, along with a frisson she could not explain. There was guilt that he needed his father so much that he imagined his presence, helplessness because she did not know what to do. At first, she had thought it a phase that would pass and had said little to disillusion him. Now, she wondered if she had done the right thing. Should she have nipped it in the bud from the beginning?

"She certainly can," she said. "And so can you. Why are you not asleep?"

"Papa woke me."

Deliberately, she sat at the foot of the bad, as close as she could to where he had been gazing when she first entered. For an instant, she imagined the warmth of another presence, familiar and welcome, and old grief mingled with irritation at her own weakness.

"Marco," she said gently, "Papa is always with us, in our hearts and memories. Wishing he was still alive does not make it so."

"Oh, I know that, but he is here. Right beside you."

She blinked, trying to find the right response.

"We were just laughing at how wet poor Sir George was when he arrived," Mark said cheerfully. "Papa said he looked like a fountain!"

"Well, so would you if you had walked from the village in that deluge. Although you would have been a much smaller one."

Mark grinned, then his gaze slid to the side of her. "Papa says you can't hear him."

"I can't." She sat forward, reaching out her hand to him. "Marco—"

"He wants to know if you like Sir George."

Her hand fell back into her lap. "Why don't you just ask me yourself, if you want to know?"

"Oh, I know. I can tell you like him. So do I. But Papa worries, because he is a stranger and because of the recent trouble."

Francesca deliberately smoothed out her forming frown. There had been a series of annoying tricks this last month—mostly people knocking on the door and hiding. She had blamed children, probably put up to it by their parents, either directly or indirectly. They died away when she had not reacted. Though Martin had tottered after someone into the woods.

Had the incidents worried Mark more than she had seen at the time? "Oh, we don't need to worry about such jokes," she said lightly. "And I believe Sir George is a perfect gentleman."

Again, Mark glanced away from her. After a pause, he said, "He had better be—according to Papa."

"He will be gone tomorrow," Francesca said. Surprised by the sudden stab of sadness, she focused on Mark's imagination instead, and tried a different approach. "Why is Papa here and not at rest?"

Mark's eyebrows flew up in surprise. He glanced away in silence, then back to Francesca. "He says because he didn't want to leave us. He says he is watching over us."

"He is not God," Francesca said, more tartly than she had intended, perhaps because Mark's answer did not sound like Mark. The words sounded more like…Percival's.

She shivered. Something soft trailed across her cheek, like a breath or the faintest of caresses, and her breath caught. She had felt this before, in bed, only half awake as she longed for Percival, dreamed, perhaps, that he was not dead. And for those instants, she had believed it, before reality intruded along with the tears.

Her hand flew to her cheek, but of course there was nothing there. Not physically. But her own imagination was playing tricks, for she almost sensed his presence, warm, lively, and once so very necessary…

"You must sleep," she said to Mark, rearranging the pillows and pushing him gently to lie down. He did not resist, although he smiled beyond her shoulder, and the hairs on the back of her neck stood up. She only just stopped herself from jerking around to look. "Papa would not wake you in the middle of the night."

Even as she said the words, she remembered that he had done so on several occasions, returning from a tour of concerts or just because he wanted to see his son smile at him. She wasn't surprised by Mark's skeptical look. Instead, it made her laugh.

She stroked the hair off his forehead and kissed him goodnight. Then she sat and waited for him to close his eyes and fall into the deep, even breathing of sleep. She rose silently and tiptoed from the room, leaving the connecting door slightly ajar.

As she climbed back into bed, she wondered if it was her late husband's presence she felt, or the faint excitement of guilty new interest.

SHE WOKE WITH the realization that today was Hallowe'en. All Hallows' Eve. Not that it made any difference to her life. She suspected it was merely the discussion with Mark about Percival's presence that prompted her to think of it. Though to be sure, Percival was no demon!

For the first time, it seemed, she could smile at his memory, the simple warmth of affection uncontaminated by grief. The grief would never go completely, of course. He had been her first love, and much too young to die. But for her own sake as much as Mark's, she had to return to life. Mark himself was becoming a warning of what could happen to someone too absorbed by the past and what should have been.

Since Mark was still asleep, she went downstairs alone and found Ada in the kitchen.

"Sir Arthur's gone to the village already," Ada informed her. She sniffed. "Seems like a respectable gentleman. Courteous."

"Indeed. Did he take his baggage with him?"

"No, he means to return, whether or not his chaise is repaired, to thank you for your hospitality."

This pleased Francesca far more than it should. She was glad she had chosen to wear the lavender morning gown rather than the gray, which made her look too much like the ghost she was becoming.

After breakfast, she harnessed the old pony to the trap, and she and Mark made a quick tour of the tenant cottages to make sure none had been damaged by lightning or the excessive rain. Fortunately, they found nothing worse than a couple of minor leaks, which she promised to have dealt with today.

On the way home, they halted, as they sometimes did, for a cup of tea with Mrs. Gates, whose husband rented the nearest farm and cottage. She had a daughter the same age as Mark and a son a couple of years older. They were friendly children, and for the first time, Francesca encouraged Mark to go outside and play with them. Aware of the hostility in the village, she had kept him too much away from other children, but now she realized the harm it was doing.

On impulse, she asked Mrs. Gates about the children coming to Hazel House next week. Mrs. Gates looked genuinely pleased and agreed at once.

Francesca returned to Hazel House feeling better, more hopeful that she had since Percival's death. They enjoyed a light luncheon while Mark chattered away about the Gates children.

When Mark sloped off to play with his toy soldiers in his room, Francesca cleared up and, leaving the used crockery with Ada in the kitchen, went outside through the back door to fetch water from the well in the yard. Ada could no longer manage the heavy jobs. Nor could Martin, really. Francesca needed younger servants, and preferably a few more of them, but the Martins had been with Percival's family forever, and she could not turn them out. Besides, she was fond of them, and they were loyal.

Her thoughts fled with an unpleasant jolt. Two men stood by the well, sniggering. She recognized them as Jack Forest and Bill Kell, two of the most offensive villagers. Bill held a wriggling cat, while Jack pulled up the well bucket and rested it on the wall.

"What are you doing?" she demanded, her voice sharp with both irritation and suspicion.

They were not remotely alarmed. In fact, Jack grinned. Bill seemed too concerned with holding on to the wriggling cat. With another unpleasant jolt, she recognized it as one of the stable cat's last litter of kittens.

"Afternoon," Jack said, as though he had every right to be here.

"What are you doing?" she repeated, marching closer, her own large, empty pails in either hand.

Jack looked at the bucket in his grasp. "Fetching water. You don't grudge us a drink of water, do you?"

"Is something wrong with the village well? Your own taps?"

"Long walk to the village," Bill observed with blatant insolence.

"Which makes me wonder what brings you here," she retorted. "Be so good as to release my cat. He clearly does want to be held."

"Unlike the lady of the house," Jack said slyly.

Francesca's face flamed with anger. "You will keep a civil tongue in your head when you address me."

This was where, in the past, they would laugh, as if it was just a joke, and then they would slouch off, snorting and cackling, making other half-heard comments that she always chose to ignore. But it seemed they had grown bolder.

Bill did not release the cat. Neither of them laughed. Instead, Jack took a step closer, meeting her gaze with open insolence.

"Or what?" he sneered.

Her fingers curled hard on the handles of her pails. She fought the urge to bring them up and crash them into his head, for in doing so, she would lose what was left of her dignity, admit they could hurt her. In truth, there was nothing she could do, and she could think of nothing to say. She had never felt so helpless in her life.

And they knew it. They saw it.

"Well?" Bill said. He came closer, too, the cat still in his grasp. Jack's grin broadened. "What *are* you going to do?"

"Ma'am," said an unexpected male voice, causing Francesca and the men to jerk their heads around in surprise.

Sir Arthur Astley, George to his friends, dismounted from the back of a strange horse at the stable door and, abandoning it, strolled toward the well. Francesca's heart thudded with relief to have an ally, or at least a distraction.

"What?" Bill said, clearly confused, if not quite frightened.

"What are you going to do, *ma'am*," George corrected him with apparent patience. "One treats a lady with courtesy."

He continued toward them, a distinguished figure, although Francesca would never have called him an imposing one—until now. He held the attention of both the other men. The cat, taking advantage of Bill's distraction, lashed out suddenly with her claws and broke free with a yowl, shooting back toward the safety of the stable.

"A *lady*," Jack muttered, not quite beneath his breath. Clearly, he did not respect George either, which infuriated Francesca.

"Yes, a *lady*," George snapped, holding his gaze. "And what the lady does is none of your business unless she chooses to tell you. What you do, on her property, however, *is* Mrs. Hazel's business. And I believe she requested your immediate absence."

As he walked past the men, not quite brushing against Jack, Francesca found herself holding her breath. But no one tripped or jostled him. His manner was too authoritative. He stopped beside Francesca, facing them.

Jack and Bill exchanged glances, and seemed to take courage from it, for Jack sneered openly once more. "So the question is for *you*? What are *you* going to do about it? What *can* you do?"

"In the short term, I really don't advise you to find out. In the longer term, I suspect a consultation with my old friend Mr. Paston will be productive."

Mr. Paston was the local magistrate, though how George had discovered it was beyond Francesca's current ability to imagine.

Again, Jack laughed. "What are you going to charge me with? Stealing a bucket of water?"

"How could I?" George replied. "There is no water in the bucket. I was thinking more along the lines of attempted murder."

Francesca set down her pails. Jack and Bill stared at him open-mouthed.

"What were you planning?" George asked. "To put the poor cat in the bucket and lower it into the well so that it cried and frightened the household for Hallowe'en? And if the creature drowned, the well would be poisoned."

The idiots had clearly not thought of that. For the first time in their encounters, the fear was on their side, not hers.

"Rot!" Jack said aggressively. "I was just having a drink!"

"From an empty bucket?" George inquired. He turned his gaze on Bill. "And you?"

Bill swallowed. A trickle of blood ran down his cheek where the kitten had scratched him. "I like cats," he said lamely.

"They clearly don't like you," George observed with apparent amusement. "You may go, and do not return without invitation."

There was a short, surprised silence. Then Jack pushed the bucket off the wall and slouched away, Bill at his side. Jack tried to give a laugh of bravado as he went, but it was a poor effort.

CHAPTER FOUR

While Francesca, dazed, watched them go, George wound the well bucket down to collect water. He was pouring it into the bucket at her feet before she found her voice.

"Thank you."

"How long has their harassment been as bad as this?" He didn't look at her but lowered the bucket into the well once more.

She swallowed. "They have never been so blatantly threatening before."

"I hope I have not made it worse. I wanted to frighten them a little, shock them back into some semblance of reality."

She frowned. "How do you know Mr. Paston?"

"Never met him in my life, though I do intend to speak to him. I discovered in the village that he is the magistrate. Have you spoken to him before?"

"About those two and their ilk? And charge them with what? Calling me names?"

"There are suitable laws," George assured her.

"I would rather it did not come to that. I have to live here. And their families have to live."

"Not at the expense of yours," George said, unloading the second bucket and returning it to the well. "They are bullies of the worst kind. But a word of warning from Mr. Paston should be enough. They think you are alone and unprotected."

I am. Worse, she was Mark's only protection. She shivered. "Perhaps my pride has got in the way. And Mrs. Paston is a friend of the vicar's wife."

"Who insulted you in the first place."

Both her pails were filled now. He covered the well and, as she bent to lift the buckets, he picked them up instead.

She walked beside him with a murmur of thanks. Her hands were shaking. "They were frightened of you."

"Not at first." He gave a quick, rueful smile. "Jack was in the inn last night when I asked for a room. I did not cut a brave figure."

"You certainly made up for it this afternoon," she said warmly. In fact, she began to see the funny side of the encounter. "I have never seen anyone so haughty, so perfectly, politely, in command."

"I learned it from a friend of mine who plays the supercilious nobleman to perfection. Of course, he *is* a nobleman, which helps."

She laughed, and he smiled back. Unexpected happiness surged through her. What a shame he would leave. She would never see him again. But she would never regret knowing him.

"How is your chaise?" she asked.

He wrinkled his nose. "The wheelwright is busy on it. It will not be ready today. Apparently, the inn can supply a replacement vehicle, but not before tomorrow morning. By which time, I hope my own chaise will be ready. But at least the inn is emptying. I can have a room there tonight."

"Or you may stay here," she blurted, glad only that he would not leave today. She cleared her throat. "Mark will be glad of your company."

※

WAS IT POSSIBLE she would be too? He had been appalled by the threatening behavior of those two louts by the well, and in truth, he was reluctant to leave her without resolving the issue with some certainty.

He had seen how shaken she was, how helpless. The louts had seen it too, unfortunately. He only hoped his own intervention had been enough to convince them she was *not* helpless. Or unprotected.

Accordingly, after a quick cup of tea and detailed directions, he remounted his hired horse and rode up to Paston Hall, where he sent in his card with a request for an immediate interview with the magistrate.

He was shown at once into the study, where Paston welcomed him with every courtesy. He was a distinguished man of middle years, a little self-important in his speech, perhaps, but attentive and clearly concerned that a gentleman traveler should be in need of his services.

"It is not really on my own behalf I have come," George said, settling into the chair he was offered. "I was merely forced by a carriage accident to stay in the village last night. You may or may not have been aware that a prizefight took place in the vicinity this morning?"

Mr. Paston blushed slightly, and George said at once, "No, no, that is not my complaint. My problem was merely that there were no rooms available at the inn, and some of the locals directed me—maliciously, I now suspect—to Hazel House. In my naiveté, I imagined it to be a lodging house of some kind, not the private residence of a gentleman's widow and her child."

"Ah," Mr. Paston said. "I trust Mrs. Hazel has not caused you offense?"

Goerge felt his jaw drop. "*Mrs. Hazel*? Of course not. Because of the storm and my own semi-drowned condition by the time I got there, she felt obliged to give me shelter. Sir, my concern is that I was sent there as some kind of trick. These tricks seem to have become a habit with certain elements within the village. What is more, those same people subject Mrs. Hazel to insult and inuendo on an almost daily basis. And they are growing bolder."

"Mrs. Hazel's reputation—" Paston began apologetically.

"Is being slandered daily," George interrupted. "I am aware of it. I doubt you can be, sir, for I am aware the lady has made no complaint to you. However, when I returned to the house this afternoon, with the intention of collecting my baggage and removing to the inn, I found two of the same villagers who had sent me there last night, in the midst of some ploy or other. They seemed to be trying to put Mrs. Hazel's cat down the well in her yard, no doubt with the aim of frightening her. And when she attempted to send them about their business, their manner was undoubtedly threatening. I hate to imagine what might have happened had I not arrived on the scene."

"I'm sure you are worrying unnecessarily," Paston said, with just a shade of anxiety. "Who were these men?"

"One Jack Forest and Bill Kell, I believe."

"Ah. Wastrels, to be honest. But not dangerous, I assure you."

"I hope you are right," George said at once. "Because I very much doubt that if your wife was left a widow—God forbid—you would like to think of her being harassed, insulted, and jostled by such apparently non-dangerous wastrels."

Paston blinked rapidly. George could almost see him weighing what he knew against the gossip of his wife and, hopefully, imagining her in a similar situation. Certainly, he looked alarmed for the first time. George pushed his point home.

"As you know," he said mildly, "the fact that she once played music on the stage does not deprive her of the protection of the law. My own feeling is that the matter need not progress to formal complaints if informal steps are taken now. If they are not, I fear a genuine tragedy that will affect the whole community."

Again, Paston looked startled. He licked his lips. "These men *are* bullies," he replied. "I'll have a word with them and with a few others tomorrow. It should be enough."

"Thank you," George said. "I believe it will be." He rose to his feet. "Ordinary people often follow the lead of their betters. Perhaps if the local gentlemen's wives were to call on her and include her occasionally…"

Mr. Paston looked appalled.

"Ah. You have forbidden your wife from calling on Mrs. Hazel?" George said innocently.

"Of course not," Paston said, looking genuinely shocked. "My wife chooses her own friends, and I have never interfered. In fact, when Hazel was alive, he and his wife dined here more than once."

And the fact that she had clearly not been invited since would not have been lost on the villagers.

Paston must have realized that, for he cleared his throat. "Thank you for bringing the matter to my attention."

"I believe Mrs. Hazel was too proud to ask for your help. But I could not in all conscience leave the area without making you aware of her plight."

"When do you leave us, sir?"

"Tomorrow, when my chaise should be fully repaired. In the circumstances, I shall stay tonight at Hazel House. My faith is in you to quash any unseemly rumors of my reasons."

"Oh, quite, Sir Arthur. Quite."

George offered his hand. "Good day!"

Mr. Paston gravely shook his hand.

⁂

BY THE TIME George came back, Francesca had pulled herself together, able to concentrate on the humor of the confrontation at the well rather than on her own terrible feeling of powerlessness.

He came in through the kitchen, as if he had known that was where she would be. It was odd the way her mood instantly brightened, not only with relief but with a curious sense of ease, as if now everything was right. It was not, of course. He would leave tomorrow.

"Paston will have a quiet word in the first instance," he said at once. "He might even persuade his wife to call upon you later. I doubt you wish to be friends with her, but you should probably accept her for the good of your reputation in the neighborhood. She owes you that much and more."

Francesca laid down the knife with which she was cutting vegetables and wiped her hands on her apron before pulling it off. "How did you manage that?" she asked cynically.

"I think I got him to consider his own wife in such a situation. I have found that many people lack the empathy to imagine themselves in another's position. I used to be one of them. I have learned. Others can too. To some, of course, it is an inconvenience because they wish to believe someone *less* than they are. I call it dehumanizing."

Francesca sank onto the nearest stool, indicating he should sit also. He did, and Ada brought them each a cup of tea before retreating to her stove.

"I have become inhuman?" Francesca asked, wondering if she should be offended.

"To people like Jack and Bill, yes. Probably also to the vicar's wife and Mrs. Paston, even Mr. Paston. They will have convinced themselves that because you once played on the stage you are not respectable and are therefore unworthy of normal, human consideration. It is not right, but it happens."

Something in his voice made her peer more closely. "Did it happen to you?"

His eyes slid away. But he nodded. And then he moved his gaze back to hers, as though with conscious bravery. She wanted to take his hand and assure him he was one of the finest human beings she had ever met.

He said, "As a child, I did not always understand what was expected of me. And no one seemed to understand me. Except my little brother. My father thought I was stupid, then mad. Then one day he explained to me that Hugh, my brother, would make a better heir to his land and title. I believed him and promised to help Hugh in every way I could. In due time, my father died and Hugh inherited according to plan. I was happy to help him make the land profitable, and to invest wisely and cleverly on the Exchange. It was only gradually that I realized he was taking everything, and I had nothing but two rooms and a garden in the house that should by rights have been mine."

Francesca set down her cup. "But that is monstrous and surely illegal!"

George smiled sadly. "I had become less than human to my brother. I was a tool, a machine, to be guarded but not cared for."

"What happened?"

"I had little to do but read. I longed to see the world I learned of in books, to meet people other than Hugh and his wife and our old nurse. Hugh and Caroline had ambitions too, and to further them, he hired a lady, ostensibly to be a companion to Caroline but really to help look after me so that they could go away together for longer periods of time. That lady, Hera, became my first friend. The man she married, a doctor, was my second. They helped me to see my worth and to understand that *I* was the better man to have the land and the title. So I took them back."

She searched his eyes, aching for the pain of betrayal he must have suffered, admiring the spirit that had made him into the assured, gentle man who sat across the table, quietly drinking his tea in her kitchen.

"Good," she said. "And you are telling me this because I should take back control of my life, too?"

"The situations are different. But I would like to help you in any small way I can. As Hera helped me."

"You already have," she said, through a peculiar tightness in her throat.

He poured some more tea from the pot into both their cups. "I have another confession."

"You have?"

He cast her a slightly crooked smile. "When I was in the village this morning, I posted a letter to some friends in London. It is possible you will receive a visit from the Duchess of Cuttyngham. She is Hera's sister-in-law. You should not look surprised if she greets you as though you are old friends."

After a stunned moment, she began to laugh. "You are like a fairy godmother! Or should I say godfather?"

"Neither, if you please," he said, and she laughed harder—which might have accounted for the tears she had to wipe from her face.

<hr>

DINNER WAS A very pleasant meal. They dined early so that Mark could join them, but the autumn nights were drawing in and it was already dark. Ada and Martin both served at a very slow pace and then departed, leaving them to help themselves thereafter.

"I think you need younger servants," George observed.

"We might be able to afford them this year," Mark piped up, with no concept of discretion, repeating only what Francesca had once said to him. "Then Ada and Martin can retire with a pension."

"I see. Very proper," George said, leaving her to wonder what on earth he made of it in reality. But he changed the subject, and the rest of the time was spent in lively conversation and laughter.

Afterward, Francesca took Mark upstairs to bed.

"You will write to me, won't you, sir?" Mark said anxiously from the drawing room door.

George, who was pouring himself a glass of brandy, at Francesca's invitation, glanced at him. "Of course I will. But we will meet again in in the morning."

Mark grinned and allowed himself to be led off. "I like Sir George," he confided on the stairs. "Do you?"

"Yes, very much."

"That is what I told Papa. He likes him too, now."

Francesca glanced at him doubtfully, wondering how she should respond. "Why?" she asked at last.

"Because he stood up for you."

"When?" she asked.

"At the well this afternoon."

Mark had not seen the incident at the well. She knew from Martin, who had been tending to the bedroom fires at the time, that Mark had been playing in his own room at the other side of the house.

"Who told you about that?" she asked.

"Papa, of course."

A ripple of unease twisted through her. Could something of Percival really have remained here after all? She wanted him to be resting in peace.

Yet as they entered Mark's room, it struck her that her late husband's presence, even if only in memory, had grown stronger in the last few days. In Mark's imagination and her own. Which was odd when Sir George was here and causing her to think of so many other possibilities in her life.

When she returned to the drawing room, George was seated with his brandy on the table beside him, a book open on his knee. He rose at once, asking if he could fetch anything for her. She smiled and shook her head. The evening would pass all too quickly without addling her wits with more wine. And tomorrow he would go. An ache within her intensified and spread.

Eager to learn all she could of him, she asked him more about his life, his estates in Lincolnshire. She was intrigued to learn he had been in Brussels during the Waterloo campaign and met the Duke of Wellington himself. He did not dwell on the aftermath of the great battle where so many had died, but she gathered he had played his part in transporting the wounded and that the experience still pained him. Having seen something of war herself, she understood.

Deliberately, he lightened the conversation, but she could think of nothing to say except, *"Tomorrow you will be gone and I will be lonely again. It will be so much worse than before, because now I have known you."* And she could not say that. How could she even believe it herself when she had known him barely twenty-four hours?

Silence stretched between them. She wanted to break it yet was afraid of saying something stupid just to keep him here, something that would betray her sudden vulnerability. But somehow, his presence was so comfortable that her tension eased and she simply enjoyed his silence.

"I have to thank you for another delightful evening," he said at last, rising to his feet. "In fact, for all your kindness."

"Nonsense. You have returned any kindness tenfold." She stood also, facing him with too much space between then. "May we not simply be friends?"

She was slightly hurt when he appeared to think about it before answering. "Simply, I doubt," he said. "But friends, most definitely." His sensitive mouth twitched into a half-smile. "I would like us to meet again."

Her heart beat faster. "So would I," she admitted, and his smile broadened. She caught her breath.

She wanted him to take her hand. She wanted to touch him, kiss his cheek, anything to show friendship, to bring them closer. She knew instinctively that he would not take advantage. And he would not touch her.

Before she could gather her courage, he murmured, "Goodnight." Then he bowed and walked away, much as he had done last night. It seemed a lifetime ago.

Restlessly, she moved toward the piano, and the urge to play overwhelmed her. She wanted to express this sudden emotion and soothe it at the same time. And it was better than thinking, even with her nerves jangled.

She sat on the stool with something of a bump, instantly spreading her hands across the keys, and began to play, letting her fingers go where they willed. After a little, she fell into Beethoven's *Moonlight Sonata*, and played her heart out. She knew it was for him, even if he could not hear her.

But someone was listening. She felt the presence, the shadow in the doorway. For an instant, she wondered if it were Percival haunting her for her faithlessness. But of course it was not.

It moved, and she stopped abruptly, stumbling to her feet, staring at George as he crossed the room. Even before he came to a halt right in front of her, she could see the admiration in his eyes, the dancing spark of excitement and knowledge. As though he had read her feelings in the music.

She had always played from the heart.

Her throat constricted. She had not realized quite how beautiful his eyes were, or how expressive. For such a gentle man, his naked feelings were fierce, melting her very bones. And that was before he even touched her.

When would he touch her?

His eyes devoured her, settled on her mouth, and butterflies cascaded through her stomach. She could not breathe for the thrill of hunger, of need. She did not even know if it was his or her own.

Why did he not speak?

Because his eyes said everything. The man had always communicated with his eyes, and she doubted many people ever noticed. She did, and it consumed her.

Very slowly, he lifted one hand and brushed his fingertips across her cheek, a soft, wandering caress. His parted lips quirked into a smile.

What would his kiss feel like? It would be sweet, so sweet, so...*necessary.*

His hand fell away. He took a step backward, turned, and strode out of the room.

Chapter Five

By the time she climbed into bed, Francesca realized it was not lack of desire that kept him from her but respect for her situation. George would never take advantage. He was that rare breed, a true gentleman. And in the peace of her own bedchamber, reflecting on the disrespect she had received from the villagers since Percival's death, she was grateful. His care made her feel precious.

And yet her body clamored for love. Even while the rest of her rejoiced at the emotion within her, and within him. She smiled and closed her eyes, meaning to think of him a lot more before sleep claimed her.

However, she fell asleep almost at once, and dreamed not of George but of Percival.

He stood at the foot of her bed, managing to look both sad and excited as he did when he was leaving her for a few days or weeks. She smiled back because she understood he would be happy for her. He would want her to move forward with her life, find renewed happiness. He would have done the same had she been the one to die.

She was content with that, though sad because she had loved him so much, and he was never coming back.

And then everything changed. The curtains of the bed burst into flames, and Percival was no longer smiling but shouting at her.

"Francesca! Fran! Francesca!"

She could not move. She was paralyzed by sleep.

"Francesca! Can't you see the fire? Get *up!*"

She woke with a gasp, her heart hammering. Of course the bed was not on fire, but she could still imagine she smelled smoke, heard the crackling of flames. A quick glance showed her the guard still before the smoldering embers in the fireplace. But the sense of urgency, of panic, remained.

She leapt out of bed, pulled back the curtains, and opened the shutters to peer out of the window. An ominous glow came from the end of the house.

"Dear God," she whispered.

She bolted across the floor, pausing only to shove her bare feet into slippers and seize a shawl from the end of the bed before dashing through the connecting door to Mark's room.

She touched his shoulder, forcing herself to shake him gently. A panicked child would be less easy to control. "Marco, wake up, sweetheart. We have to leave the house for a little. Come, out of bed."

With shaking hands she forced slippers onto his feet and seized him by the hand before snatching the night lamp. "Take your coat," she said as they passed it hung on the back of a chair. She had no hands free to carry it for him.

George. She had to wake George.

※※※※

GEORGE HAD NOT meant to fall asleep. He had lain down on his bed fully clothed, smiling because he had read the beginnings of love in Francesca's eyes, and she was a happiness he had never thought possible.

Afterward, he never knew if it was dream or reality, but a man he knew was Percival Hazel was shaking him. "Fire," he shouted. "It is up to you to save them!"

With a jolt, reality swamped him. The smell of burning, the bright orange glow through the window he had not shuttered, the sound, surely of cracking flames. And not in his hearth. That fire had gone out. He leapt up, seizing the still-burning lamp from his bedside table, and burst out into the passage. He ran toward the main stairs to bang hard on Francesca's door.

From here, he could see the smoke billowing downstairs. And on this floor, further toward the servants' stairs. He was just about to burst into Francesca's room when she emerged from the next door along, grasping Mark in one hand and a small lamp in the other.

"George!" she cried in relief. "We must get out! I don't know how bad it is…"

"Stay with me," he said grimly, and led the way down the stairs. Increasingly, smoke made him cough, but at least there seemed to be a clear path to the front door.

"Oh, God, Ada and Martin!" she exclaimed.

"Where are they? Where do they sleep?"

"Downstairs, the room to the left of the kitchen—"

"Hopefully they're outside already, but I'll make sure. You take Mark straight out and well away from the house."

To his relief, she did not argue. Mark had to be her first concern. Already starting toward the front door, she cried out over her shoulder, "Be careful, George!"

The desperate concern in her voice spurred him on through the baize door. Here, the smoke almost choked him. No wonder. The kitchen was ablaze, especially to the right, blocking the way to the back door into the yard.

Ignoring that for now, he located the room off the kitchen's left-hand side. Noticing a towel, he dunked it in the pail of water he passed, and burst into the old couple's bedchamber. He peered through the thick smoke, raising his lamp and holding the wet towel over his nose and mouth.

They lay side by side, perfectly still.

<hr/>

FRANCESCA THREW BACK the bolts of the front door. They felt warm, as though the whole house was heated by direct sunshine. She wrenched open the door, still grasping the silent Mark by one hand, and all but staggered into the open.

Even the outside air stank of smoke, and she could see at once that one side of the house was in flames.

"Oh dear God," she whispered. She grasped Mark's hand more tightly and ran down the path toward the garden.

"There! Undressed!" a gleeful voice cried out of nowhere.

Startled—could it be help arrived from neighbors?—she halted and peered at the two men on either side of the old oak tree, behind which they had apparently been hiding.

"What d'you expect?" the second man said derisively. "It's the middle of the night. The question is, is *he* in his nightclothes too? And you must admit, he ain't with her."

Francesca stared at them, her jaw dropping. It was Jack Forest and Bill Kell. "You are betting on the fire in my house? Instead of helping?" she said in disbelief. "My son could have died! My servants, whom you have known all your lives, still might." *George. Oh God, George...*

And then, seeing Jack's forceful nudge before they backed away, another, even uglier suspicion hit her.

They had started the fire.

As a bet to see if she and George emerged together as lovers. And no doubt as revenge for the thwarting of their well trick this afternoon.

"Dear God," she whispered with utter contempt.

<hr/>

MARTIN SAT BOLT upright like a stage ghost, without using his hands. And coughed.

Flooded with relief, George could hardly speak. "Fire, Martin. We have to get out. Wake Ada."

The room was already unbearably hot and the old couple all but overcome. There was no time or strength to search for other exits. George made a swift decision and broke the window, battering the glass out, so that it would not cut them to ribbons.

"Hello!" shouted a voice outside. "Anyone in there?"

"The Martins!" George gasped back as loudly as he could while struggling to breathe. "I'll pass them out to you!"

Only Ada's choking sounds told him she was still alive. He picked her bodily from the bed and passed her through the window. Somewhere, he registered that it was the innkeeper from the village who took her at the other side. Martin staggered toward him in his nightshirt, and George hefted him over the sill. Eager hands took the old man from his grip. Hastily, George dragged the covers off the bed and pushed them through, too. They would be needed.

The fire was spreading rapidly toward him, licking under the bedchamber door. From long-ingrained habit, George doused the lamp he had earlier set on the dressing table, and laughed at himself as he jumped and threw himself through the window.

Helping hands caught him, dragging him away from the heat of the building. He could see the old couple, wrapped in blankets, and several local people, including the innkeeper and the blacksmith. Desperately, he sought Francesca and Mark, but he could not speak to ask.

And then, like a whirlwind, she landed in his arms, sobbing, "Oh, thank God, thank God!" And for one blissful moment, her lips pressed to his cheek, his mouth, and his arms closed hard around her.

It was only an instant before he realized the innkeeper and his wife were subtly sheltering them from view. Which at least brought enough sense back to George to draw her away from him.

"Mark?" he said urgently.

"Safe with Mrs. Gates. You brought the Martins out alive, George, thank you!"

And then she fled toward the Martins, who might have been alive but were still struggling to breathe.

George realized that the hands helping him away from the building belonged to Mr. Paston, the magistrate.

"Thank God you're all safe," Paston said fervently. "I'll never forgive myself for not warning those two today as I should! If I had not thought to tell the constables to patrol past the house tonight, it could have been so much worse."

George wrestled his foggy brain into understanding. He stared at Paston. "You are saying the fire was started deliberately?"

Paston nodded. "By Forest and Kell. Not with intention to injure, I'm sure. They're just too ignorant to realize how quickly a fire can spread. I believe the aim was to see if you and Mrs. Hazel emerged together. A stupid, dangerous wager. And yet if you hadn't been there, the Martins would be dead."

George shivered with memory, gazing toward the burning house. It would never recover from this. All Francesca's married life, her home and her son's, were burning to the ground. Had some shade of her husband really warned him? If he had not, would George ever have awakened? Would Francesca or Mark have?

"Where are they?" he asked Paston with rare savagery.

"In custody. They'll be locked up until charges are brought."

George swallowed. His throat felt as if was full of hot razers. "Does Mrs. Hazel know?"

"Most of it. You must all come up to Paston Hall. My wife is expecting you, and the doctor has been summoned there."

Paston was tugging him toward a carriage. But George could not help looking back at the blazing house. Was the remnant of Percival

Hazel still there? Peering hard, he could almost imagine a ghostly figure in the flames.

Thank you, he mouthed silently.

And it seemed as if a voice answered directly into his head. Almost an echo. *Thank* you.

Chapter Six

THE AIR WAS still thick with smoke the following morning when Francesca returned to Hazel House. What was left of it.

That the consequences could have been so much worse did not incline her to forgive Jack and Bill for what they had done. Under no circumstances was it acceptable, whatever the damage or whoever did or did not die. She would have nightmares forever about losing her son, her servants, and her friend to such a horrendous death. And so she had told Mr. Paston, who seemed more than happy to see the pair charged with arson and the attempted murder of five people.

As she gazed at the still-smoldering ruin of her home, she still did not weep. She was too shocked and angry. But she walked inexorably toward it. She guessed nothing could be salvaged, but it hardly mattered beside the hugeness of the saved lives.

She had left Mark warily getting to know one of the Pastons' grandchildren. She had not seen George since last night, when they had met, numbly, in the Pastons' house, before being led away to different baths and clean beds and the ministration of the local doctor. But she knew George was well enough to go into the village. Perhaps he had left already in his repaired post-chaise. She could hardly blame him. His journey home had gone from bad to worse.

She surveyed the wreckage of her home. Among the blackened rubble she could recognize the odd piece of furniture, a few ivory keys from the piano, a piece of molded plaster from the drawing room, a mantelpiece, a miraculously survived Venetian glass vase.

Something caught her eye, and she climbed over a pile of mostly stable stones to get to it. She picked it up slowly. Another miraculous survival. The broken neck of Percival's violin, strings hanging loose.

She suspected it had not been burned in the fire but stood on by those who had tried so hard in the beginning to put it out. Which for some reason seemed even sadder.

She sat slowly down on the stones, still holding the piece of instrument in her hand. It grew blurry before her eyes.

"Your poor, beautiful violin," she whispered, and discovered she was weeping after all—for what had happened and what might have, for Percival and her home, for her own loneliness, and the pointless, reasonless hatred that had brought about this whole mess.

Something brushed against her cheek. She knew his touch as she knew her own. "I'm sorry," she gasped. "Percival, I am so sorry."

For an instant, it felt like his arm around her, and she had to look. It might have been swirling smoke, but it looked like him. Her hair might have blown around her lips, or he might have kissed them. But he was not sad. He was glad.

And abruptly, so was she. He was going at last to his rest. Not because fools had burned his home but because she was strong enough to cope. And she was. She knew that. And yet still she wept and wept. She didn't know for how long, until a strong, much more solid arm came around her, and she turned into George's chest with a deep, low sob.

He sat beside her in silence, holding her, stroking her hair until the storm passed.

"He has gone," she said into George's neck. "He woke me last night because of the fire, and now he has gone."

"May he rest in peace. Do you mind?"

The question was asked so carefully that she raised her head, tear stains and all, and searched his face. "You don't think I am mad?"

"I think he woke me, too. He trusted me to help. And Mark has been chatting with him since I arrived."

"And before," she admitted. She met his gaze and finally answered the question. "No, I don't mind. I am glad because he has gone where he should be."

He nodded. "You loved him very much."

"I did." Raising her hand, she touched his cheek. He had shaved recently and did not smell of smoke, just of soap and cleanliness and George. "My life is not over. Even for this—*especially* not for this."

Somewhere not too far away, birds were singing. She could hear cattle lowing and chickens making a racket. She wondered vaguely what had happened to hers.

George said, "Do you think you might ever love again?"

"Yes," she said softly. "I think I might."

His breath caught. "Do you think that you might ever fall in love with *me*?"

Her heart thudded. "You might try to convince me."

He smiled with his lips and his eyes, and then just with his eyes as he bent his head and finally kissed her mouth.

The kiss was everything she had imagined and more. Gentle and sweet and tender. She clung to his lips, and when it ended, she kissed him back, and this time it was lazily sensual, exploring, arousing.

"Sir George," she whispered against his lips. "I have not known you two days, but I think I am already half in love with you."

"Good," he said. "For I might be wholly in love with you."

"How will we know?"

"A little more kissing might help."

It did.

Two days later, Mrs. Paston was "at home" to her gently born neighbors. Whether because of Francesca's misfortune or Mr. Paston's influence, she was now distantly kind to Francesca. If not friendly, she was at least hospitable in a condescending sort of a way. Francesca, grateful for the roof over her head and Mark's, and delighted that it was the same roof that currently harbored George, did not resent the condescension. It was a sort of truce.

Naturally, since the Hazel House fire was the main topic of speculation in the village, the "at home" was well attended. Francesca was there, and the guests were quite avid to see her. She was sure they were disappointed to find that she and George sat on opposite sides of the room, but they asked innumerable questions.

She repeated several times that the hall was completely ruined, that she and Mark had been unharmed in the fire, and that the Martins were slowly recovering, having been rescued by Sir Arthur Astley. And yes, Jack and Bill were bound over to stand trial. The vicar's wife listened without actually speaking to her. The vicar himself had called on her the day before with his sympathies and good wishes.

A footman entered once more and presented Mrs. Paston with a visiting card on a silver salver. She picked it up, blinked, and blurted, "The Duchess of Cuttyngham! Of course, show Her Grace in at once."

Francesca's gaze flew to George's face, but he was deliberately not looking at her.

"You are acquainted with the duchess?" the vicar's wife asked with a gasp.

A war waged visibly across Mrs. Paston's face, but reluctant truth won out. "Why, no, though I suppose Cuttyngs is not so very far away..." She rose to greet her august guest, nervously smoothing out her skirts.

An instant later, two young, fashionably dressed ladies swept into the room. The first lady held out her hand as she approached Mrs. Paston, who curtseyed before taking the hand in a bemused kind of way.

"Your Grace is most welcome. I am Mrs. Paston."

"Olivia Cuttyngham," said the duchess informally. "My sister-in-law, Lady Hera Rivers. I hope you will forgive the intrusion, but I have been searching for my friend, Mrs. Hazel, and just learned that her home has burned down! Could you possibly direct me to her?"

Francesca was stunned. She had forgotten George's plan, which hardly mattered now.

"But of course," Mrs. Paston said, clearly torn between shock at discovering Francesca's connection to a duchess, and delight at being able to oblige Her Grace. "Mrs. Hazel is staying with us while she decides the best way to go forward."

Now George was looking at Francesca, his gaze oddly commanding. With an inward shrug she rose and went to Her Grace. "How pleasant to see you, Duchess," she said. "I should have written to you…"

"Oh, stuff," said the duchess graciously.

"Lady Hera," Francesca murmured, curtseying also to George's first true friend, who was eying her with rather sharp curiosity. Nevertheless, she smiled and shook hands as though they too were old friends. "And Sir Arthur is here, too!"

"George, how delightful!" Hera said, going to him at once. "I didn't see you, standing there so quietly."

The duchess caught Francesca's gaze and, shockingly, closed one eye. "I've come to rush you away, my dear! Bring your lovely little boy and come with us to London for a fortnight. After which, Hera wishes to bear you off to Lincolnshire. I might come too, if Cuttyngham is willing. A fresh start, I think?"

The vicar's wife's jaw seemed about to hit the floor. She had publicly and frequently insulted the friend of a duchess. Mrs. Paston began to look smug.

"Perhaps you have an announcement, George?" Lady Hera said

clearly.

"Actually, I do. Mrs. Hazel has agreed to be my wife." George smiled directly into Francesca's eyes, and she smiled back with all the love and all the laughter surging inside her.

"You *see* him," Lady Hera said in surprise. "You really do see him for what he is."

"I love him for what he is," Francesca said proudly, and the happiness in George's face dazzled like the sun in winter.

The End

About Mary Lancaster

Mary Lancaster lives in Scotland with her husband, three mostly grown-up kids and a small, crazy dog.

Her first literary love was historical fiction, a genre which she relishes mixing up with romance and adventure in her own writing. Her most recent books are light, fun Regency romances written for Dragonblade Publishing: *The Imperial Season* series set at the Congress of Vienna; and the popular *Blackhaven Brides* series, which is set in a fashionable English spa town frequented by the great and the bad of Regency society.

Connect with Mary on-line – she loves to hear from readers:

Email Mary:
Mary@MaryLancaster.com

Website:
www.MaryLancaster.com

Newsletter sign-up:
http://eepurl.com/b4Xoif

Facebook:
facebook.com/mary.lancaster.1656

Facebook Author Page:
facebook.com/MaryLancasterNovelist

Twitter:
@MaryLancNovels

Amazon Author Page:
amazon.com/Mary-Lancaster/e/B00DJ5IACI

Bookbub:
bookbub.com/profile/mary-lancaster

Printed in Great Britain
by Amazon